Princess Cora
and the
CROCODILE

Princess Cora and

the CROCODILE

LAURA AMY SCHLITZ

illustrated by
BRIAN FLOCA

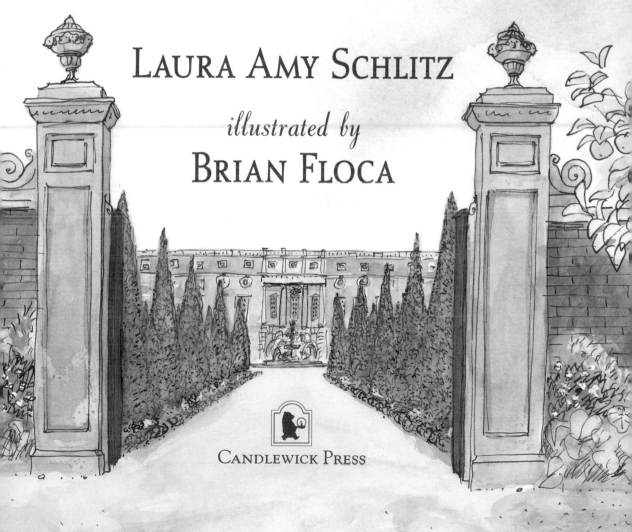

CANDLEWICK PRESS

Text copyright © 2017 by Laura Amy Schlitz
Illustrations copyright © 2017 by Brian Floca

First edition 2017

Library of Congress Catalog Card Number pending
ISBN 978-0-7636-4822-0

16 17 18 19 20 21 CCP 10 9 8 7 6 5 4 3 2 1

Printed in Shenzhen, Guangdong, China

This book was typeset in Diotima.
The illustrations were done in ink, watercolor, and gouache.

Candlewick Press
99 Dover Street
Somerville, Massachusetts 02144

visit us at www.candlewick.com

To Twig,
with love and a crocodile
L. A. S.

To
Esme and Helene
and Daria and Jonathan
B. F.

Chapter One

When Princess Cora was born, her mother and father thought she was as perfect as a snowflake.

"Look at those big blue eyes!" shouted the King.

"Look at her toes!" cried the Queen, and she kissed the baby's feet. "They're like pink pearls!"

"Someday our little girl will be Queen!" said the King.

All at once the Queen looked worried, and so did the King, because blue eyes and pink toes would not help Princess Cora to rule the land.

"We must teach her," said the Queen.

"We will train her," said the King.

So that very day the King and Queen began to train Princess Cora. They stopped thinking she was perfect and started worrying about what might be wrong with her. By the time she was seven years old, there wasn't a single minute when Princess Cora wasn't being trained.

The King and Queen hired a nanny to make sure that Princess Cora was always tidy. The nanny thought that being clean was the most important thing in the world. She made Princess Cora take three baths a day and watched like a hawk to make sure she washed herself all over.

"Into the tub you go," the nanny would say, "and scrub-a-dub-dub till I say stop!"

Sometimes Princess Cora got tired of taking baths. But the nanny always shook her finger and said, "Do you want to be a dirty little girl? Do you want to smell bad?"

Then Princess Cora turned red and took another bath.

5

When she wasn't taking baths, Princess Cora studied hard. Every day she went to the tower room and read books about how to run the kingdom.

"A princess must be wise," said the Queen.

The books were so dull that Princess Cora yawned until her eyes were full of tears. Sometimes she asked silly questions, just to liven things up. Then the Queen frowned an awful frown and said, "Now, Cora, that is inappropriate!"

So Princess Cora hung her head and went back to work.

After she studied, Princess Cora went down to the old castle prison, which the King had turned into a gym. Every day the King stood with his gold watch in his hand while Princess Cora ran in circles and skipped rope up to five hundred.

"Faster! Faster! A future queen must be strong!" said the King. "Skipping rope is good for you!"

Princess Cora knew that skipping rope was good for her, but that didn't make her like it any better.

Sometimes she tried to say so, but when she did, the King squatted down in front of her and made his face look very sad. He said, "Princess Cora, are you being a good girl?"

Princess Cora knew it would be of no use to say *yes*, and she didn't want to say *no*. So she burst into tears.

Princess Cora wanted her parents to be happy. She worked hard at being clean and strong and wise. But deep inside, she was angry. Sometimes at night, when she was alone in bed, she whispered, "Skipping rope is stupid! And I'm sick, sick, sick of those boring books! When I grow up, I'm never going to take any baths. I'm going to be *dirty*!"

These thoughts scared her, but she couldn't stop thinking them.

One night a new idea crept into her head. It was different from the others, because it was a happy thought. She whispered, "What if I had a dog?"

She smiled in the darkness. She thought of a great, furry, golden dog that would wag its tail and jump on her. A dog wouldn't tell her what to do. "That's what I want," whispered Princess Cora. "A dog!"

But when she told the nanny, the nanny cried, "A dog, a dirty dog! A dog would make messes on the carpet! Good heavens, you don't want that!"

And the Queen said, "Dogs are for little girls who have time to take care of them. I'm afraid you're too busy, dear."

And when Princess Cora asked the King if she could have a dog, he stared at his gold watch and shouted, "Faster! Faster!" because she was trying to talk and run in circles at the same time.

That night Princess Cora couldn't sleep. At last she got out of bed and wrote a letter to her fairy godmother.

Dear Godmother,

Nobody listens to me. My mother and father won't let me have a pet and Nanny says I don't even want one. But I do. And I'm sick and tired of everything.

Please help me.

Love,

Princess Cora

Then she tore the letter into scraps
and dropped them out the window.
But because it was a letter to her
fairy godmother,
every scrap turned into
a white butterfly and
flew
away.

Chapter Two

$\mathcal{W}$hen Princess Cora awoke the next morning, she found a box at the foot of her bed. There were holes punched in the top so that something inside could breathe.

Princess Cora lifted the lid. Inside was a scaly green animal with a pink bow around its neck. "Goodness!" cried Princess Cora. "An alligator!"

The animal smiled. He had teeth hanging down from his top jaw and more teeth poking up from his bottom jaw.

"Guess again!" he said.

"Are you a crocodile?" asked Princess Cora.

"I am *your* crocodile," answered the animal, "and your new pet. I've come to rescue you from your awful parents and your mean nanny."

"My parents aren't awful. And Nanny isn't *too* bad," said Princess Cora. "And I wanted—" She stopped. She'd meant to say that she wanted a dog, but she didn't want to hurt the crocodile's feelings. "Besides, how could you rescue me?"

"I bite," said the crocodile, and he opened his mouth to show all his teeth. He had so many that Princess Cora jumped and let out a little scream.

"Don't be frightened," said the crocodile. "I won't bite you. I'm your crocodile. I'll only bite people you don't like. And I won't eat

them, unless you insist. I seldom eat people. I just like to chew on them. What I really like to eat is cream puffs."

Princess Cora considered this. "I can give you cream puffs," she said. "That's one good thing about being a princess. We always have cream puffs. Do you like chocolate or vanilla?"

"Both," said the crocodile greedily, and he started for the door. Then he stopped. "Wait! I haven't saved you yet! Your fairy godmother told me to save you."

"No one can save me," Princess Cora said sadly. "Unless you can turn yourself into a dog."

"I can't do that," said the crocodile, "but I can knock people down. I swat them with my tail and they fall on their rear ends, bang! *Then* I chew on them."

Princess Cora shook her head. "I don't think that's a good idea."

"If you don't want bites, and you don't want rear ends, what do you want?" asked the crocodile.

Princess Cora thought hard. "I want a day off," she said at last. "No baths, no books, no skipping rope. Just a day to do what I like."

"I know what!" exclaimed the crocodile. "I'll take your place! I'll wear your clothes and take your baths and learn your lessons and jump over your stupid rope. Then you can run away and have fun."

"I don't think—" began Princess Cora, but the crocodile grabbed one of her dresses and jammed his back legs into the sleeves, as if he were putting on a pair of pants. "Oh, dear! Not like that!" cried Princess Cora, and she ran to help him.

In a very short time the crocodile was dressed in Princess Cora's dress. When he stood on his hind legs and hid his front claws behind his back, it was astonishing how much he looked like Princess Cora. There was just one problem.

"Your tail shows," said Princess Cora. "I haven't got a tail."

"That's not my fault," said the crocodile, but he whipped his tail out of sight.

"And there's a problem with—" Princess Cora stopped. She almost said "with baldness," but she didn't want to be rude. "Little girls have hair," she said at last.

"Make me a wig!" said the crocodile.

21

Princess Cora started to say that she couldn't. Then an idea came to her. She found her nanny's mop and took the stringy part off the stick. She tied the stringy part to the crocodile's head. The yarn in the mop was the same shade of brown as Princess Cora's hair.

"There!" said the crocodile, peering into the mirror. "Don't I look sweet?"

"You're perfect!" said Princess Cora. "Do you know, I think this might work? At least, it might work with Nanny. She never wears her glasses. And Mama's always reading. And Papa's always looking at his watch."

"Of course it will work," said the crocodile. "Now, I'll stay here and be Princess Cora, and you run along and have fun."

No one had ever told Princess Cora to run along and have fun, and she almost didn't know how. But she dressed herself in the flash of an eye and ran down the castle steps and out the back door.

The castle garden was very tidy, with trees shaped like cones. Princess Cora wanted untidy trees, the kind she might be able to climb. So she raced past the lily pond and ran into the orchard, where the fruit trees grew.

Chapter Three

When the nanny came into Princess Cora's room, she wasn't wearing her glasses. She saw the crocodile in Princess Cora's pink dress and made an angry clucking noise. "Why, you dirty little girl! Why did you get dressed when you haven't had your bath?" She shook her forefinger. "Into the tub you go, and scrub-a-dub-dub till I say stop!"

The crocodile tried to take off his dress, but his claws weren't good at undoing buttons. "Oh, never mind," he said, and took a great leap into the water. He made such a splash that the water poured over the sides of the tub.

"What a mess!" cried the nanny, and went to get her mop. She stared at the stick. Then she looked back at the tub. She saw that the stringy end of the mop was tied to Princess Cora's head, and that Princess Cora had a long green tail.

The nanny began to think that something was wrong. She cried, "Why, you're not Princess Cora!"

"Yes, I am," said the crocodile, and he sang a little song:

"I'm Princess Cora, yes, sirree!

I am her, and she is me.

I'll bite you if you disagree—

I'm Princess Cora—hee, hee, hee!"

The nanny cried, "You nasty thing!" and hit him with the mop handle. "Get out of the tub this minute!"

"All right," said
the crocodile. He leaped out of the tub,
splashing more water onto the floor. There
were puddles everywhere, and that gave
the crocodile an idea. He emptied a jar of
bath oil on top of the puddles. "Let's make
a waterslide!" he said. "Come slide with me!"

And he grabbed the nanny around the waist
and made her slide. The nanny screamed.

"Isn't this fun?" said the crocodile, and he slid
some more.

When he was tired of it, he sang out, "Bath time! Scrubby, scrubby!" He heaved the nanny into the tub. The nanny was frightened. She found it hard to scrub herself, because she was wearing all her clothes. Every now and then, she tried to climb out of the tub, but the crocodile always put her back in. Once she tried to slap him, but he shook his claw at her and gave her a little nip on the arm. After that, she stayed where she was.

"Now, you keep washing," said the crocodile, and winked at her.

While the water was growing cold in the tub, Princess Cora was looking for a tree to climb. She stood on one foot and hooked the other one over a high branch.  There she stood, stuck, because she couldn't see how to get the rest of her up to where her foot was.

At last she found a tree with a very low branch. She wiggled her bottom against the branch until she was sitting in the tree.

She stood up and began to climb. She skinned her elbow and tore her petticoats, but she didn't stop climbing until she was nine feet off the ground, with the cool green leaves all around her.

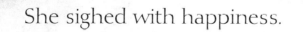

She sighed with happiness.

Chapter Four

While Princess Cora was climbing the tree, the crocodile was climbing the stairs to the tower. The Queen was reading and didn't look up to smile at Princess Cora. "Sit down, dear," she said, "and take out your pen."

The crocodile took a quill pen and dipped it in ink.

"Write down everything I say," commanded the Queen.

She read to the crocodile about money and banks. The crocodile yawned loudly, showing his sharp teeth, but the Queen didn't notice. The crocodile looked for something to play with. His eyes fell on the ink bottle. He tried balancing it on the end of his snout, but he turned out not to be good at this, and the ink flowed out, forming a great black puddle.

The crocodile sighed. He raised his eyes to the ceiling. Above his head was a glass chandelier. It hung from a silver chain. In an instant, the crocodile was up on the table. He gave a mighty leap, grabbed the chandelier, and began to swing back and forth.

The Queen heard the glass tinkle. She frowned when she saw Princess Cora's dress, swinging like a bell above her head.

"Princess Cora," she began, "that is *most* inappropriate! Come down from there this minute!"

Then she stopped. She had seen the crocodile's feet, which were webbed, with four sharp toes. "You're not Princess Cora!" cried the Queen.

"Yes, I am," sang the crocodile. "Yes, I am!"

The Queen
wasn't fooled, not one bit.
She was a great reader, and science
books had taught her how to tell a crocodile
from a little girl. "You're a reptile!" she snapped.
"What are you doing here?"

The crocodile went on swinging. His green tail
swept the tabletop, smearing the spilled ink.

He sang:

"I am Princess Cora's pet—
Am I her favorite croc? You bet!
Inky-stinky, dry or wet.
And I am inappropriate!"

The Queen couldn't stand
this. "That's a bad rhyme!"
she shouted. She picked
up a fat book and threw
it at the crocodile.
"Reptile!" she yelled.

The crocodile caught it and
tossed it back. "Mammal!"

The Queen didn't
like being called
a mammal. She
cried, "Guards!" and
rushed for the door,
but the crocodile took
a flying leap and got there
before she did. He snapped his teeth
at her. Then he chased the Queen around the
tower until she was dizzy. When she fell down,
the crocodile nipped her, once on the left ankle,
and once on the right ankle.

"How dare you?" said the Queen. "It's against the law to bite the Queen!"

"Crocodiles don't have laws," said the crocodile.

The Queen grabbed the nearest chair and tried to hit him.

"That is *so* inappropriate," said the crocodile. He took the chair from her and bit it. Then he tossed the pieces away and went out, locking the Queen inside the tower.

While the Queen was shouting for the guards to unlock the door, Princess Cora was kneeling in the orchard, picking strawberries.

The strawberries were redder than rubies and smelled like roses and honey. Princess Cora filled her skirt with them. Then she opened the gate and went into the woods.

There was a great pine tree with branches that swept the ground. Princess Cora crept under it and ate strawberries until her teeth were full of tiny seeds.

Then she began to build a fort. She took off her petticoats and used them for the roof. She scooped up brown pine needles to make a bed. Once the bed was made, she lay down and sniffed the piney smell of the needles.

But she was too happy to sleep. The sound of trickling water reached her ears, and she got up to follow it. When she found a little creek, she took off her shoes and stockings and dipped her feet in the water. It was so cold that her toes stung.

She waded for more than an hour.

The stream led her into a pasture full of cows and buttercups. While she was picking buttercups in her bare feet, Princess Cora stepped on a cow pie.

It was the most disgusting thing that had ever happened to her. Princess Cora hopped up and down on one foot and squealed, "Ew, ew, ew!"

Then she stopped and thought and said proudly, "I'm having an adventure," and wiped her foot on the grass.

Chapter Five

$\mathcal{W}$hile Princess Cora was being brave about the cow pie, the crocodile was crawling down the cellar stairs to see the King. He found the King running in place with a weight in each hand.

"Late again!" panted the King. "Quick, pick up your rope and skip to five hundred! I'll count for you!" He put down the weights and took up his gold watch.

The crocodile sighed. He was beginning to get tired of Princess Cora's family. He picked up the skipping rope, swung it over his head, and hit himself in the ankles. "Ow!" he said.

The King never took his eyes off his watch. "Start over!" he shouted. "Faster this time! A princess must be quick and strong!"

The crocodile tried again, but crocodiles are not built for skipping rope, and the rope got stuck under his tail. He lost his temper.

"I hate skipping rope!" he yelled. "And I'm not going to do it anymore!"

The King was so surprised that he dropped his watch. He went to the crocodile and squatted down before him.

"Princess Cora," he said in the sad voice that Princess Cora hated most, "are you being a good little girl?"

The crocodile threw down the skipping rope. He yelled, "I don't want to be a good little girl! I want to be a bad crocodile. And what's more, I *am* one!"

Then the crocodile tore off his dress. The King was so shocked that he put his hands over his eyes.

"Princess Cora!" he shouted. "What are you thinking! No matter what happens, *we do not take off our clothes!*"

"Yes, we do," said the crocodile, grinning. He lunged at the King and caught the King's trousers between his teeth. There was the sound of ripping cloth. The King squealed and put his hands over his rear end.

"Princess Cora!" cried the King. "Behave yourself!" But the crocodile only snapped his teeth.

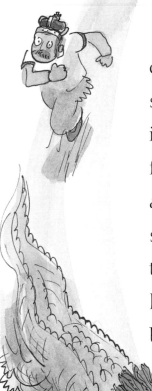

The King began to run. The crocodile rushed after him, shouting, "Faster! Faster!" And indeed, the King ran very fast. But no man is as fast as a crocodile, and after the seventh lap around the gym, the crocodile lashed his tail, knocked the King down, and began to chew on him.

It struck the King that his daughter's teeth were very, very sharp. He saw that his daughter's nose was long and scaly and green. The King cried out, "Good heavens! You're not Princess Cora!"

"Am too," said the crocodile, but it sounded more like "mmmtttfff" because he was chewing. It wasn't easy to chew on the King, because he had such strong muscles. His rear end was tough, like dry bubble gum.

"Ouch! Help! Crocodile!" cried the King. He pulled free and dashed toward the steps. The crocodile made a lasso from the skipping rope and threw it over the  King's head. Then the crocodile tied up the King, binding him with double knots.

The King howled with rage. His rear end was wet with crocodile spit, and he hated being tied up. But it did no good to howl, because the gym had once been a prison, and the walls were very thick.

The crocodile slithered up the stairs, shut the door, and locked it. "There! That's done! One in the tub, one in the tower, and one tied up all right and tight. What a day! But Princess Cora will be happy. She'll want to give me one thousand hundred cream puffs."

His mouth began to water as he thought of those cream puffs. He slunk out the back door to wait for Princess Cora.

At that very moment, Princess Cora was walking by the lily pond. She'd lost her shoes somewhere by the creek, and her dress was covered with strawberry stains. She felt very peaceful. She stopped to admire the water lilies in the pond. It was a large pond, with a splashy fountain. Princess Cora bent over it and washed her hands. She thought of how angry the nanny would be when she saw the stains on her dress. "But I'll say I'm sorry," she told herself, "and I'll tell them all why I ran away. Perhaps I can make them listen, if I am very polite and tell the truth."

When she reached the castle door, she found the crocodile waiting for her. His wig hung beside his left cheek, and he had no dress on.

"What happened?" asked Princess Cora.

"They didn't believe I was you," said the crocodile. "So I bit them."

"You bit them!" said Princess Cora. "I told you not to!"

"I forgot," said the crocodile. "But don't worry. They'll get over it. Your nanny shook her finger at me—"

"Ooh, I hate that," said Princess Cora, "but you shouldn't have bitten her."

"She got on my nerves," said the crocodile, "so I stuck her in the tub. After that, your mother read to me about banks, but I couldn't stand it. She said I was inappropriate."

"She says that to me, too," said Princess Cora, "and it's awful. You didn't bite her, did you?"

"I did," said the crocodile. "Twice."

"Twice!" cried Princess Cora.

"She has two legs," said the crocodile. "Then I locked her in the tower."

"You didn't!" said Princess Cora.

"Well, I did," answered the crocodile. "And then I told your father I didn't want to jump over that stupid rope, and he asked me if I was being a good girl. It was the way he said it. *Anyone* would have bitten him. But he wasn't even fun to bite. He's the wrong kind of chewy. Your family's horrible. I don't know how you put up with them."

Princess Cora frowned at him. "I never said you could hurt them," she said. "I told you not to bite. Now I'll be in trouble, and I've never been in trouble my whole life."

"What kind of life is that?" asked the crocodile.

Princess Cora shook her finger at him. "You're a bad, bad crocodile," she said sternly, "and—and inappropriate—and you've made everything worse."

The crocodile burst into tears. He covered his eyes with his front claws. "You're mean," he sobbed. "Mean, mean, mean! You told me not to eat anybody, and I didn't, even though I'm starving to death. And you said I could have cream puffs, and I haven't had any, not one single cream puff! And now you're mad at me!" The crocodile writhed and kicked. He lashed his tail. "I wish I was dead!" he moaned, and he rolled over and over in his grief.

Princess Cora's heart melted. She took out her handkerchief to wipe away the crocodile's tears, but he kept his claws over his eyes and wouldn't look at her.

"Poor Crocky," she said gently. "You were never cut out to be a princess." She patted his snout. "Don't cry. Poor old Crocky-dilly, you never had your cream puffs."

The crocodile peered out from behind his claws. "This is what I'm *telling* you," he said. Quick as a wink he sat up, like a dog begging. "How about it, then? How about some cream puffs?"

Princess Cora laughed. "Oh, come along," she said. "I'll feed you, and then I'll try to fix everything."

Princess Cora led the crocodile into the kitchen. "Cook," she said, "will you give this crocodile some cream puffs?"

The cook was surprised to see the crocodile, but she had just made six batches of cream puffs with chocolate on top. "I'll feed him," said the cook, "but he mustn't bite me."

"Did you hear that?" Princess Cora said to the crocodile. "No bites."

"Right-o," agreed the crocodile.

Chapter Six

Then Princess Cora went upstairs and found her nanny, who was still in the bathtub.

"Princess Cora!" the nanny cried. "Thank goodness you're here! A bad crocodile bit me and frightened me to death! I am so cold, and so wet, and so sick of being in the tub!"

"Oh, poor Nanny!" cried Princess Cora. "Let me bring you a towel."

Princess Cora helped the nanny take off her wet clothes. She found her a warm nightgown and buttoned her up the back. "Poor Nanny!" she crooned. "Now you climb in bed and get warm! I must go and see Mama."

She ran up the stairs to the tower. When she unlocked the door, the Queen cried, "Oh, my dear Princess Cora! Thank goodness you're all right! A dreadful crocodile was here, pretending to be you! He bit me and chased me and locked me up with nothing to read but these boring books!"

"Poor Mama!" said Princess Cora. She ran for towels to wipe up the ink. She brought soap and water and a clean bathrobe, because the Queen's gown was all spattered and spotty. Princess Cora tried to get the ink off the books, but the Queen seized the stack of books and flung them out the window.

"Mama!" said Princess Cora. "What are you doing?"

"I'm throwing these books away," answered
the Queen. "I've been locked up with them for
hours, and they're deadly dull!"

Princess Cora tried not to smile. "Yes, they
are," she agreed, and kissed her mother. "Now
I must go and find Papa."

When Princess Cora opened the cellar door, the King moaned most pitifully and held up his tied-together hands.

"Oh, dear! Poor Papa!" cried Princess Cora. She knelt down and began to loosen the knots.

"Oh, Princess Cora," groaned the King. "A wicked crocodile chased me and tore my pants—no, don't look!" cried the King. "Shut your eyes!"

"How can I untie you if my eyes are shut?" asked Princess Cora.

"I mean, don't look in back," said the King. "That crocodile tore a hole in my pants!"

"Oh, my goodness," said Princess Cora, and she fetched her father's bathrobe and covered him up. Then she untied all the double knots.

When the King was free, he stood up and stretched. "Now what?" he said. "There's time to skip rope before supper."

"I think we should have supper now," said Princess Cora. "I'm hungry." And she was, because strawberries are not very filling, and she had run up and down a great many steps.

Chapter Seven

So Princess Cora and the nanny and the King and the Queen had supper together. The grown-ups were all in their bathrobes, and Princess Cora still had pine needles in her hair, but everyone was too hungry to care. Nobody spoke until after dessert, which was cream puffs.

Then the Queen said, "We must hunt down that crocodile and get rid of him."

"Yes," said the King. "Then we can go back to the way things were."

Princess Cora felt her heart beat fast. "He's not such a bad crocodile," she said. "My fairy godmother sent him to me. I like him."

"Like him?" said the Queen.

"That nasty, dirty crocodile?" said the nanny.

"The one who tore a hole in my pants, and chewed on my rear end, and got crocodile spit on my behind?" said the King.

"Yes, I do," said Princess Cora. "And there's something else I have to tell you." Her heart beat even faster. "I don't want to go back to the way things were before. Please, please, listen to me."

The King and the Queen and the nanny were listening. They looked shocked and a little angry, but they were listening. And this time Princess Cora didn't hang her head or turn red or burst into tears. She had climbed a tree that day, and built a fort, and stepped on a cow pie. Those things had made her brave.

So she spoke up. "I'm tired of taking baths," she said. "I think three baths a day is too many. And in between baths, I'd like to get dirty. I want to play outdoors and dig in the garden."

The nanny looked upset, but the Queen only said, "Is that all?"

"No, it isn't," said Princess Cora. "From now on, I want to choose my own books. I want to read about sharks and tigers and fairies."

"The books upstairs *are* a little dry," said the Queen. "Is that all?"

"Not quite," said Princess Cora. "I'm sick and tired of skipping rope. I want to climb trees and roller skate and learn to juggle."

The King sighed. He shifted on his pillow, because his rear end still felt sore. At last he said, "Well, those things will make you strong. So I suppose that will be all right."

Then the King and the Queen and the nanny said, "That's all settled."

But Princess Cora said, "There's one more thing. I want a big golden dog with a fluffy tail."

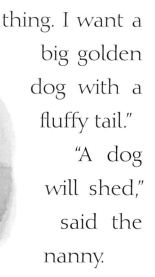

"A dog will shed," said the nanny.

But the King argued, "Walking a dog will make the Princess strong."

And at last the
Queen said, "After all,
a dog is better than
a crocodile." So they
agreed that Princess
Cora could have a dog.

"May I have two
dogs?" asked Princess
Cora, but the Queen said,
"Don't push it." So Princess Cora said, "One
dog will be lovely." And she kissed them all.

"Of course,"
they said, "you
must give up
the crocodile.
Crocodiles do
not belong in
castles."

"I understand,"
said Princess Cora.

So the very next day Princess Cora got a lovely golden dog with a fluffy tail. And her life changed. She took only two baths a day, and in between them she got dirty. Some days she read law, and some days she read fairy tales. Some days she skipped rope, but other days she skipped skipping rope. And every day she walked her golden dog by the lily pond, where they ate cream puffs together.

And every day Princess Cora threw a dozen
cream puffs into the water . . .

just in case there was someone
there who liked them.